I0746610

Preface

This series of books has been produced for the enjoyment of both children and adults.

They seek to raise awareness of the value of the relationships between pets and people and demonstrate how having a pet enriches your life and family.

Proceeds from the sale of the books will go towards supporting people and pets, by endeavouring to:

🐶 Change the world for one dog at a time with our Rescue, Rehoming   and Retirement Program,

🐶 Bringing lonely pets and empty laps together with our Cuddles and Co Program.

🐶 Keeping pets and people together with our Paws and People Boarding and Assistance Program – and

🐶 Paying It Paw-ward with our Program that provides financial assistance to people with pets who are struggling financially.

Introduction

In our first book, The Hope Springs Gang, (often referred to as just "The Gang") we introduced you to our troop of small fluffy dogs who live on a little farm in a beautiful place with their family – the Dogmother and the Dogfather.

In this book, we meet Dug and Scarlett – two foster dogs who met each other in their foster home with Bec, Andrew, Peyton (and later, Sadie). Both Dug and Scarlett had lots of attitude and didn't like anyone outside their family. But when Dug met Scarlett - it was love at first sight – and that's a scandal they don't want anyone to find out - in fear that it will ruin their fearsome reputations!

Dug is a Chihuahua. He came to live with Mum Bec, Dad Andrew, and Miss Peyton about three years ago when he needed to find a new home.

Though Dug is small – he is a Dude with a big a-ti-tude! His family call him the Spicy Burrito (amongst other names).

Dug doesn't like ANY other dog! He tells them what he thinks of them in no uncertain terms.

Dug does however, like rolling in smelly stuff. The smellier the better! This results in Dug needing lots of baths – and sometimes he needs the purple horse shampoo to get rid of the stink!

Dug loves his food – so much so that he's become some-
what 'loaf' looking!

On Christmas Eve when the family left carrots out for the reindeers and a cookie and drink for Santa – Dug was sure the food and drink was for him!

Dug also loves his unicorn – and simply must have it to go to bed or take a nap!

Dug loves his little person, Peyton and joins in her games.

Most of all – Dug loves his Mum! Well – he did – until – Scarlett came to stay!

Now, Dug loves Scarlett most of all!

Scarlett is also a very small chihuahua. She has an attitude though – that just might be bigger than Dug's!

Scarlett didn't have a very good life before coming to live with Dug and his family and as a result she is VERY afraid of a lot of things! When little dogs are afraid, they think if they bark and growl and look scary – people won't hurt them.

Scarlett likes curling up on the back of the lounge where she is high and feels super safe.

Scarlett doesn't like anybody else – but - she does love her family!

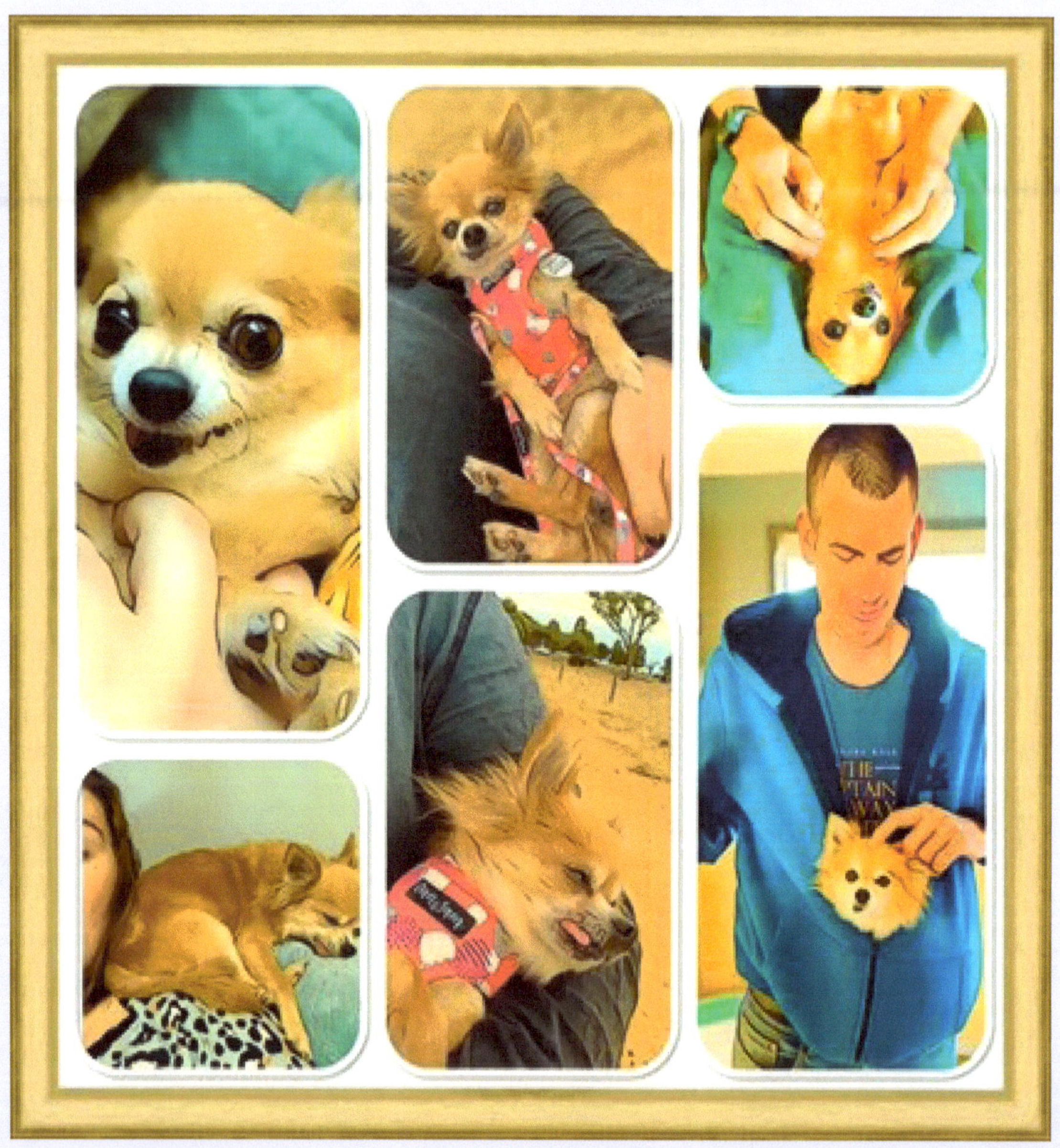

Dug adores Scarlett and even let her have his special yoghurt treat!

Dug and Scarlett like to play together – and when they're done – they like to curl up and snooze together!

Dug and Scarlett like playing games and having training sessions with Miss Peyton

Dug and Scarlett are like two peas in a pod or like peas and carrots – they just go together! So, it makes sense that they get married so they can stay together!

And here is the whole Scandalous Scanlan family before baby Sadie came along!